Pet Friends Forever

Problem Pup

by Diana G. Gallagher

illustrated by Adriana Isabel Juárez Puglisi

capstone

is published by
Picture Window Books,
A Capstone Imprint
1710 Roe Crest Drive
North Mankato, Minnesota 56003
www.capstonepub.com

Library of Congress Cataloging-in-Publication Data
Gallagher, Diana G., author.
Problem pup / by Diana G. Gallagher; illustrated by Adriana Puglisi.
pages cm. -- (Pet friends forever)

Summary: Kyle's friend Drew has adopted a dog from the shelter, but the
boys need to teach it manners and obedience or Drew's parents are going
to send it back.

ISBN 978-1-4795-2176-0 (hardcover) -- ISBN 978-1-4795-3802-7 (pbk.)
-- ISBN 978-1-4795-5232-0 (ebook)

1. Dogs--Behavior--Juvenile fiction. 2. Dogs--Training--Juvenile
fiction. 3. Dogs--Juvenile fiction. [1. Dogs--Training--Fiction. 2.
Dogs--Fiction. 3. Pet adoption--Fiction.] I. Puglisi, Adriana,
illustrator. II. Title.
PZ7.G13543Pr 2014
813.6--dc23
2013028614

Designer: Kristi Carlson
Image Credits: Shutterstock/Kudryashka (pattern)

Printed in China.
092013   007749WAIMANS14

TABLE OF CONTENTS

1

Clinic Chaos

"C'mon, Rex!" Kyle called as he ran down the street toward his mom's veterinary clinic Friday afternoon.

Rex, Kyle's yellow Labrador retriever, ran beside him, leaping and turning in circles. Rex could sense that Kyle was excited, so he was excited, too.

Kyle yanked open the front door of Dr. Blake's Veterinary Clinic and hurried inside. Practically bursting with excitement, he pulled a paper out of his pocket. He couldn't wait to show his mom how well he'd done on his math test.

Behind the counter, Lillian, the clinic's receptionist, smiled at him. "You look like you're in a good mood," she said.

"I am," Kyle said. "I got a hundred percent on my math test!"

"Congrat—" Lillian started to say. But just then, Rex came charging past Kyle into the waiting room.

"Look out!" Lillian shouted.

Rex's leash got tangled around Kyle's feet, making him lose his balance. Kyle fell against the magazine rack, knocking it to the ground with a loud *CRASH!* Papers scattered across the floor. Rex yelped with surprise and jumped away, knocking into a cat carrier on the floor. The cat inside hissed angrily.

Across the room, a small poodle was waiting with its owner. The dog pulled against his leash and yapped at the cat. His front feet came off the floor when he barked, and he squeaked when he landed.

Angry hisses continued to come from inside the cat carrier. Finally, the cat's owner picked up the carrier and put it on his lap. He shot an irritated glance at Kyle and Rex.

The little poodle continued yapping and tugging at his leash to get free.

"Bailey, no!" the poodle's owner said, pulling the little dog away.

Everything seemed to be calming down a bit . . . then Rex started barking. The poodle immediately looked at Rex and jumped out of its owner's lap. Rex dropped into a play bow on his front end.

"Bailey! Get away from that animal right now!" the woman holding the poodle's leash hollered.

"Sorry!" Kyle said, grabbing Rex by the collar. "He won't hurt him. He just wants to play."

The poodle suddenly seemed to realize that Rex was bigger. The little dog turned tail and scrambled to safety between his owner's feet.

Rex thought the poodle was playing. He jumped toward the little dog.

"Get away!" Bailey's owner hollered again.

Lillian came out from behind the front desk to stand between the two dogs. "It's okay, Mrs. Stone. Rex won't hurt Bailey," she said. She glared at Kyle. "But he's being a very bad dog today!"

Kyle tried to pull Rex back. "Stop it, Rex!" he said firmly. "Come here."

But Rex wanted to play with his new poodle pal. He didn't budge.

Just then, Kyle's mom came walking into the waiting room. "What is going on out here?" she demanded.

"That dog attacked Bailey," the poodle's owner said, pointing at Rex.

"No, he didn't!" Kyle protested. "He just wanted to play!"

"Outside, Kyle," Dr. Blake said. She pointed to the front door and gave her son an irritated look. "Now!"

Bailey started yapping all over again, and Kyle had to drag Rex out the front door. His mom followed, closing the door behind her. The noise in the waiting room immediately quieted.

"Now what happened?" Dr. Blake asked.

"It wasn't Rex's fault, Mom," Kyle said. "I knocked over the magazine rack. And the cat started hissing, and the poodle started barking, and Rex wouldn't shut up. But he wasn't trying to hurt that dog. He just wanted to play."

Dr. Blake sighed and rubbed her forehead. "Kyle, we've talked about this. What are the Rex rules?" she asked.

Kyle's shoulders sagged and he looked at the ground. "That Rex has to behave when he's in the clinic," he mumbled.

"*All* the time," his mom said. "No exceptions. That means no barking and no playing with the patients. I can't have him upsetting people."

Kyle nodded. "I know," he said. "Sorry, Mom."

"I think it might be a good idea if Rex stays away from the clinic for a while," Dr. Blake said. "If there's another incident like this, he won't be allowed in the clinic at all."

Dr. Blake went back inside the clinic, and Kyle turned to walk next door to their house. Rex trailed along next to him quietly. He seemed to sense he was in trouble.

As they walked into the kitchen, Kyle remembered his perfect math test. He was still holding the paper, but it didn't seem that exciting anymore. Rex was in big trouble with Mom. And that meant Kyle was, too.

2

Bad Dog Fix-It Plan

A few minutes later, the doorbell rang. Kyle opened the door and saw Mia, his best friend and next-door neighbor, on the porch.

"Hey, Mia," Kyle said. "What's up?"

"I was hoping you and Rex would want to go to the park with me," Mia said.

"Sure," Kyle replied. "Come on in while I grab my shoes and coat."

The two kids made their way to the kitchen, where Rex was lying on the floor. He looked over at Mia and Kyle when they walked in, but he didn't move.

"What's wrong with Rex?" Mia asked. "He looks depressed."

"I think he knows he's in trouble," Kyle explained. "He went a little nuts at the clinic."

"What did he do?" Mia asked.

Kyle sat down to pull on his shoes and told Mia what happened. "If Rex messes up again, he'll be banned from the clinic for good," he finished. "My mom was really mad."

"Maybe Rex just wasn't in the mood to listen," Mia suggested.

Kyle sighed. Rex wasn't in the mood to listen a lot of the time. Especially if he was busy chasing squirrels. Or eating. Or smelling something. Or napping. "You need to remind him that you're the boss," Mia said.

Kyle nodded. "You're right," he said. "He already knows all the obedience commands."

"But he only does them when he feels like it," Mia pointed out. "He has to do them when you say so."

"All the time," Kyle agreed. "Even if a squirrel kicks him in the nose!"

Mia giggled. "Or it rains dog treats."

"Or he smells pizza," Kyle said. "When I say *come*, I mean it!"

Rex's ear twitched when he heard the command, but he didn't sit up to obey.

Mia sighed. "You've got a lot of work to do," she said.

"No kidding," Kyle said. "So let's get started."

Kyle grabbed Rex's leash, and the three of them headed to the dog park. He usually let Rex relax and check out all the doggy-delicious smells along the way, but today, he made the yellow Lab heel and stay by his side.

Rex wasn't happy about it. He kept trying to veer off the sidewalk to sniff the trees. Every time Rex pulled on his leash, Kyle made him stop and sit for a minute. After the fourth stop, Rex finally gave in and walked nicely.

The dog park was extra crowded by the time they made it there. There were dogs catching Frisbees, digging in the sand, and rolling on the grass. Two black Labs dashed through tunnels and leapt over jumps on the agility course. A few tired dogs napped under benches while their owners read or talked on cell phones.

"Wow!" Mia exclaimed when they entered the fenced playground for dogs. "There must be fifty dogs here today!"

"Maybe more," Kyle said as he looked around. "I've never seen it this crowded before."

"Are you sure this is the best place to practice?" Mia asked.

"It's perfect!" Kyle said. He stopped, and Rex sat down next to him.

"But there's so much going on here," Mia said.

"That's why it's perfect," Kyle said. "I have to teach Rex to ignore the other stuff and just listen to me."

Just then, a man with a German shepherd ran by. Rex whined, wiggled, and started to stand up. He wanted to run, too.

"Sit!" Kyle ordered.

Rex whined again, but he stayed sitting.

"Good boy," Kyle said. He pulled a treat out of his pocket and fed it to Rex. "Okay, let's get started."

Kyle tugged lightly on Rex's leash to get the dog's attention. Then he dropped the leash and held his hand in front of Rex's face. "Stay!"

Kyle walked a few feet away, then stopped and turned around to face Rex. The dog was still sitting where Kyle had left him. But when he saw Kyle looking at him, Rex stood up again.

"Stay!" Kyle called. He held his hand out toward the yellow Lab. Rex quickly stopped moving and stood where he was while Kyle walked over.

"Sit," Kyle said as he picked up the leash again. Rex sat, and Mia applauded.

"That was great!" a boy's voice said.

Kyle glanced over and saw Drew Martin sitting on a nearby bench. A white spaniel with big black spots sat on the ground near his feet. Drew went to their school, but he was in a different fourth-grade class, so Kyle didn't know him very well.

Mia walked over to pet Drew's dog. "What's his name?" she asked.

"Lucky," Drew said. He nodded toward Rex. "Can he do any other tricks?"

"Sure," Kyle replied. He had Rex lie down, stay, and shake. Rex must have been in the mood to listen. He didn't make any mistakes.

Feeling more confident, Kyle tossed a stick a few feet away. "Leave it!" he told Rex before the dog could run after it.

Rex stared at the stick. He whined softly, but he didn't move to get it.

"Good boy!" Kyle said proudly. He knew how hard it was for Rex to resist running after the stick. He was lucky to have such a well-behaved dog.

Suddenly, Drew's dog sprang to his feet, rushed forward, and grabbed the stick. Rex immediately barked and chased after Lucky. That was Rex's stick!

"Lucky!" Drew shouted. "Put that down!"

But Lucky didn't listen. He took off running, holding the stick proudly in his mouth. Rex chased him, and the two dogs ran in circles around the park. Every time the boys and Mia tried to catch them, they raced away again.

"Rex!" Kyle called to his dog. "Come back here! Now!"

But Rex seemed to be done listening for the day. He ignored Kyle and kept chasing after Lucky.

Mia sighed. "Rex was doing so well!" she said, shaking her head.

"It's my fault," Drew said. "I was so busy watching you that I forgot to hold onto Lucky's leash. You're a good dog trainer, Kyle."

"Not good enough," Kyle said. "If Rex doesn't start listening to me, my mom will never let him back in her clinic."

"I wish that's all I had to worry about," Drew mumbled.

"What do you mean?" Mia asked.

"I've been begging for a dog for years,"
Drew explained. "My parents finally decided I
was old enough to take care of one, so they let
me adopt Lucky from the shelter a few months
ago."

"That's good, isn't it?" Kyle asked.

"Yeah, except we didn't count on getting
a dog that digs in the trash, chews up shoes,
and doesn't come when he's called," Drew
explained. He looked upset. "I've been trying to
train him since we brought him home, but it's
not working."

"Well, it takes time to train a dog," Kyle
pointed out.

"I know," Drew said, "but if Lucky doesn't learn to behave, I'm worried that my parents are going to make me get rid of him."

"What?" Mia gasped.

Drew nodded unhappily. "That's what my dad said yesterday," he told them. "He was really upset. He said that if Lucky doesn't start to show some improvement by next Saturday, he's gone."

Not if we can help it, Kyle thought. "Why don't you and Lucky meet Rex and me here on Saturday," he suggested. "I have to work on his training anyway. We can work on Lucky's at the same time."

"That would be great!" Drew said, sounding grateful. "I need all the help I can get!"

3

The Misty Mystery

Rex walked quietly on the way home, but Kyle knew it was mostly because he was tired after his game of keep-away with Lucky.

"I can't believe Drew's parents would make him get rid of Lucky," Mia said.

Kyle nodded. His mom might be annoyed with Rex, but she'd never get rid of him. "Maybe Drew's parents just don't understand dogs," he suggested.

"At least Drew wants to learn," Mia said. "Hopefully you can help him since you're training Rex anyway."

"I hope so," Kyle said. "Lucky's bad habits can be fixed. It'll just take time."

"I wish Misty's bad habits could be fixed," Mia said with a sigh. "She's been worse than ever lately."

"Worse?" Kyle said. That was hard to believe. Mia's cat, Misty, never listened. She was so mean she could chase dogs out of the yard and take down skateboarders. Once she'd even dropped a live beetle in Mia's cereal bowl.

"It's too bad cats can't be trained like dogs," Mia added.

Some can, but not Misty, Kyle thought. Misty did what she wanted when she wanted, and nobody argued.

"What's she doing now?" Kyle asked.

"Last night at dinner she crouched under my chair and clawed at my feet," Mia said. "She wouldn't stop, so we had to lock her outside until we finished."

Misty clawed Kyle's feet all the time. But going after Mia was new.

"And yesterday afternoon she shredded the mail," Mia said. "All my mom's catalogs have holes in them. She was *not* happy."

"Has Misty ever done that before?" Kyle asked.

Mia shook her head. "No. I don't know why she's doing it now."

"Maybe she's just bored and trying to get more attention," Kyle suggested.

"Maybe," Mia said. "Let's go to Mr. J's and get her a new catnip mouse. She loves those."

Mr. J's Pet Haven had been in business for thirty years. Kyle and Mia didn't shop anywhere else for dog and cat supplies. Some things were cheaper at the big chain pet store, but Mr. J knew all his customers by name. And no one knew more about pets.

A bell chimed as Kyle and Mia pushed open the door to Mr. J's Pet Haven. "Don't want any!" Jethro, Mr. J's parrot, squawked as soon as they walked inside.

"Hi, Jethro!" Mia said. "What's up?"

The bird let out a whistle and bobbed his head. "I'm hungry!" he said.

Mia picked up a cracker from the bowl on the counter and held it out to the bird. "Here you go," she said.

Jethro took the cracker with his beak and swallowed it in one bite. As soon as it was gone, he squawked, "Get lost!"

Kyle smiled. The parrot used to live at Mr. J's house. He'd learned to talk by listening to Mr. J's kids.

"That bird is such a brat sometimes!" Mr. J said with a laugh. "What brings you two in today? Anything I can help with?"

"I need a new catnip toy for Misty," Mia said. "And some treats. She's been acting a little weird lately."

"Weird how?" Mr. J asked.

"Clawing at my feet and ripping up the mail," Mia said.

"Some animals get cranky when they get older," Mr. J suggested. "Could that be it?"

Mia shook her head. "Misty isn't old," she said. "She's only four."

"Besides, she was born cranky," Kyle added. "We think she might just be bored."

"That could be it," Mr. J said. "It's hard to tell sometimes since our pets can't tell us what's bothering them. We have to figure it out."

Kyle and Mia followed Mr. J to the back of the store where the cat supplies were kept. He quickly gathered up Misty's new toy and treats.

"Why do some dogs chew stuff and play with trash?" Kyle asked.

"All puppies chew," Mr. J said. "Owners have to teach them that dog toys are okay and everything else is not. And training takes time. Some people don't want to be bothered."

Maybe that's why Lucky's first owner took him to the shelter, Kyle thought.

"And dogs can get into the trash for a lot of reasons," Mr. J continued as they walked back to the front of the store. "Sometimes dogs get nervous when they're left alone. Trash keeps them busy and calms them down."

"Rex used to get into our trash," Kyle said. "But I don't think it calmed him down."

Mr. J laughed. "Sometimes dogs do it just because ripping up smelly stuff is fun," he said.

Lucky is definitely the smelly fun type, Kyle decided.

Mr. J rang up Mia's purchases. "I hope these help with Misty," he said.

"Me, too," Mia said. "I have to wear three pairs of socks to protect my toes when I'm sleeping!"

4

Whatever Works

When Kyle and Rex arrived at the dog park on Saturday morning, Drew and Lucky were already waiting. Rex and Lucky sniffed noses to say hello, then Kyle made Rex sit. Lucky pranced and pulled on his leash. He wanted to play.

"Did you bring any treats with you?" Kyle asked.

"Yep, a whole bag," Drew said, pulling a bag out of his pocket. "But I don't know if they'll help at all. Training Lucky might be hopeless. Every time he went near the trash last night, I told him, 'No!' but he still dragged garbage all over the kitchen."

"Well, we can't teach him to be a perfect dog in a week," Kyle said. "But we can teach him how to behave a little better."

"I don't know," Drew said. He still didn't look convinced.

"Training a dog isn't easy," Kyle said. "You'll have to be tough, and it'll take a lot of time. So we'll have to cheat a little."

"What do you mean?" Drew asked.

"Your parents won't care why Lucky stops chewing stuff and playing with trash as long as he stops, right?" Kyle said.

Drew nodded. "Right. They just want me to take some responsibility for him. But how do I get him to leave the trash alone?"

"Simple," Kyle said. "Just make sure you take the trash out every night and put an empty bag in the kitchen can. Lucky can't scatter trash if there isn't any."

"That's genius!" Drew exclaimed.

"I don't know about that," Kyle said with a laugh. "I just know from experience. That's what I had to do with Rex."

"What about chewing?" Drew asked. "I read online that using hot sauce works."

"It works on table legs," Kyle said. "I had to use it on ours when Rex was a puppy. But if Lucky is chewing on shoes, it might not be a good idea. Your parents probably don't want to put their feet in hot-sauce shoes."

"Ugh, no!" Drew made a face.

"Lucky needs some chew toys," Kyle said.

"We got him some," Drew said. "But he likes shoes and books better."

"Then you can't leave anything lying around," Kyle said. "If Lucky can't reach it, he can't chew it."

Drew scratched Lucky behind the ears. "What about coming when he's called?" he asked. "I can't do that for him."

"No, we have to trick him," Kyle said. He took a ball and a treat out of his backpack. Then he took Rex off his leash and threw the ball. "Go get it, Rex!"

Rex immediately raced to fetch the ball. Drew had a hard time holding Lucky back. He wanted to go after Rex.

"Here, boy!" Kyle yelled as Rex ran back.

The yellow Lab ran back to Kyle, sat down, and dropped the ball at his feet. Kyle checked to make sure Lucky was watching. Then he gave Rex a treat.

Lucky whined.

"You'll get one, too, Lucky," Kyle said. "You just have to earn it. Ready to try, Drew?"

"I guess," Drew said. "But Lucky won't bring the ball back. He'll just run around with it."

"Not if Rex has the ball," Kyle explained. "Lucky will follow him. Just keep calling for him to come to you. And give him a treat when he gets to you."

"Okay," Drew said. He unclipped Lucky's leash, and Kyle threw the ball. Both dogs took off after it. Lucky got to the ball first. He picked it up and started running in a big circle around the park.

"Now what?" Drew asked, sounding frustrated.

"Keep yelling 'come!' and hold out the treat," Kyle said.

"Come, Lucky! Come here, boy!" Drew hollered.

Rex and Lucky ran and jumped for several minutes before Lucky saw the treat in Drew's hand. He immediately dropped the ball and ran to get it.

Drew fed him the treat. "Good boy!" he said happily.

Rex grabbed the ball and brought it to Kyle. He liked treats, but he liked playing fetch more.

"Let's try this again. Ready, Rex?" Kyle said.

This time, Kyle threw the ball. Rex grabbed it and ran straight back. Lucky chased after him, just like Kyle had hoped.

"Come, Lucky!" Drew yelled. "Come!"

Lucky started to run past, but as soon as he saw the treat in Drew's hand he turned and raced back to his owner.

"Make a big fuss petting him, too," Kyle said. "That way he'll know you're happy with what he did."

The boys stayed at the dog park and worked with the dogs for almost an hour. Rex had a great time playing fetch with Kyle. Lucky only came straight back to Drew half the time, but it was better than the day before. The spaniel was a lot smarter than Drew realized.

But success didn't just depend on Lucky. The dog's fate depended on Drew, too.

5

Progress Not Perfect

Drew and Kyle decided to meet at the dog park again the following afternoon. As soon as Drew walked up, Kyle could tell he wasn't happy.

"I'm an idiot!" Drew exclaimed.

"Why?" Kyle asked. "What happened?"

Drew shook his head. "I forgot to take out the trash last night," he said.

Kyle sighed. He could guess what had happened. "So the kitchen was a mess again?" he asked.

Drew nodded. "Yep. I cleaned it up, but my parents were really upset." He hugged Lucky tightly. "I don't want to lose him. I'll have to do better tonight."

"Maybe you could write it on your hand," Kyle suggested. "Or set an alarm to remind yourself."

"That's a good idea," Drew said. "I'll try that. So what are we doing today?"

"I'll show you some more commands," Kyle said. "But then I have to work with Rex. We'll practice getting Lucky to come later."

When Drew stood up, Lucky jumped and twisted with excitement. Drew grabbed his collar. "Down, Lucky," he said firmly. "Sit down!"

"Move him to your left side," Kyle said. "That's heel. And make him sit when you're standing still."

"Heel!" Drew said. It took a few tries, but he finally managed to pull the stubborn dog around to his side. "Sit!"

Lucky barked and wagged his tail, but he didn't sit.

"Push on his back end," Kyle told him. "And when he sits, give him a treat and pet him so he knows he did what you wanted."

Drew pushed on Lucky's back end, but the dog tried to move away. He turned in several circles before finally sitting.

"Good sit!" Drew said. He quickly fed Lucky a treat.

"Now try walk and heel," Kyle said.

Lucky pranced and jumped as Drew walked him across the field. The dog didn't listen all the time, but he quickly figured out that sitting earned him a treat.

While Drew worked on getting Lucky to heel, Kyle worked with Rex. The dog paid attention and did everything Kyle asked. Kyle rewarded him with pats and praise. He had trained Rex with treats when he was a puppy, but now Rex wanted to make Kyle happy.

At least when there aren't any squirrels or poodles to distract him, Kyle thought.

Just then, Rex yanked away, pulling the leash out of Kyle's hand. He barked and charged toward a squirrel that was busy looking for food on the ground. The squirrel immediately took off for the nearest clump of trees.

"Rex, no!" Kyle shouted. He took off running after Rex.

Across the park, Lucky caught sight of the commotion and raced back toward Rex. "Lucky, stop!" Drew yelled.

The squirrel managed to escape up a tall tree, but that didn't stop the dogs. They ran around the tree, chasing each other instead.

Kyle and Drew couldn't catch them. After ten minutes, the boys collapsed on the ground.

"All that for a squirrel!" Drew exclaimed.

"Squirrels are hard to resist," Kyle said.

Before they could even catch their breath, Rex and Lucky were jumping all over them.

"It's hard to stay mad at him," Drew said. "He loves me!"

Kyle laughed as Rex licked his face. He couldn't stay mad either. Happy dogs were impossible to resist.

Kitty Crisis

I really hope Drew remembered to take out the trash last night, Kyle thought as he ran out of the house later that week. He and Rex were on their way to meet Drew at the dog park.

In just a few days, Drew's dad would decide if Lucky would be allowed to stay or have to go. Drew and his dog couldn't afford to make any more mistakes.

Kyle was in such a rush he almost didn't see Mia. She was sitting on her porch steps with her face in her hands. *Is she crying?* he wondered.

"Mia?" Kyle called as he walked over. "What's the matter?"

Mia looked up. "It's Misty. She's in big trouble. She pooped in my dad's favorite chair," she said. "And he sat on it."

Kyle bit his lip so he wouldn't laugh. It was funny, but it wasn't funny.

"Then he yelled, 'That cat is a nightmare!'" Mia wiped away a tear. "I'm really worried. What if Mom and Dad make me get rid of her?"

"They won't," Kyle said. He didn't want to miss Lucky's training session, but this was an emergency. "Maybe Misty is sick or something. Do you want to bring her to my mom's clinic? Maybe she can take a look at her and figure out what's wrong."

Mia nodded. "Good idea," she said. "Let me go get her."

It took a while for Mia to load Misty into her cat carrier. Misty was not happy about it. The clinic waiting room was empty when Kyle and Mia walked in. Only Lillian sat behind the receptionist desk.

"Does my mom have a second to look at Misty?" Kyle asked. "We think something's wrong with her."

Lillian smiled at Mia. "We've always got time for Mia's cat," she said. "Go on back to one of the exam rooms."

As they left the waiting room, Kyle realized Rex was following. His mom hadn't given the dog permission to return, but Kyle didn't want to leave Mia alone.

"Sit!" Kyle told Rex. He held up his hand. "Stay!"

Rex sat in the middle of the waiting room floor.

"Go on, Kyle," Lillian said. "I'll watch him."

Kyle's mom met them in the exam room. "What seems to be the problem with Misty today?" she asked.

"She's just crankier than usual," Mia said. "And she pooped in my dad's chair. Kyle and I thought she might be sick."

Misty hissed when Dr. Blake put her on the exam table. The vet tech held the cranky cat while Dr. Blake examined her.

"It could be that she's sick," Dr. Blake said. "Or in pain. Animals tend to act up when that's the case."

Misty tried to scratch Dr. Blake when she opened the cat's mouth. "Ah, looks like we've found our problem," she said. "Misty has an infected tooth."

"Oh, it must be hurting her!" Mia exclaimed. "I should have figured that out. I feel terrible!"

"It's not your fault, Mia," Dr. Blake said. "Animals can't tell us what's wrong. We have to guess what's going on with them and hope we get it right."

"At least now you know that Misty had a good reason for being so bad," Kyle said. "I bet your parents won't be mad anymore."

"Is she going to be okay?" Mia asked Dr. Blake.

"She'll be fine," Dr. Blake said, "but she should stay here tonight. I'll give her medicine for the pain and the infection. Then tomorrow morning I'll take out the bad tooth. She'll be back to her old self in a few days."

"Thanks, Dr. Blake," Mia said. She gave Kyle's mom a hug.

Kyle wanted to leave before his mom saw Rex in the clinic, but she followed them out to the waiting room. Rex was still sitting where Kyle had left him.

"He hasn't moved a muscle," Lillian said.

"Good dog," Dr. Blake said with a smile. She reached out and patted Rex on the head.

Yes! Kyle thought happily. He grabbed Rex's leash and hurried out before something could go wrong. He and Mia headed to the dog park, but by the time they got there, Drew and Lucky were already gone.

7

All Work and No Play

On Friday afternoon, Kyle got to the dog park early. He worked with Rex until Drew and Lucky arrived. Lucky sniffed the ground and pranced until Drew stopped. Then the dog sat and stared at Drew's pocket.

"I'm really sorry I wasn't here yesterday," Kyle said. "We had to take Mia's cat to the vet."

"Don't worry about it," Drew said. He gave Lucky a treat and scratched his ears. The dog looked up and thumped his tail on the ground. "We practiced on our own, and Lucky did great. Is Mia's cat okay?"

"She had a toothache," Kyle explained. "My mom fixed it this morning. How are things going? What happened with the trash?"

"I took it out!" Drew said. "Every time I look at Lucky I think *trash!* It works."

"Great!" Kyle said. "Is he still chewing?"

"Well, not exactly." Drew said with a sigh. "He's been good about using his dog toys — at least until last night. I didn't know dogs liked toilet paper! Lucky took a whole roll outside and toilet-papered the backyard!"

Kyle laughed. "Really?" he said.

Drew rolled his eyes. "There were streamers and gobs of wet paper all over the place," he said. "It took an hour to clean up, but he's *my* dog, so I did it. And my parents were impressed that I did it without having to be asked."

"That's good," Kyle said. "Do you think he's ready to show your parents that he can behave tomorrow?"

"Let's see," Drew said. He shortened Lucky's leash and started walking. Lucky followed along beside him.

"Heel," Drew said. Lucky hung back, and Drew had to drag him. "Come on, Lucky! Heel."

Rex stood up and barked.

"Sit, Rex!" Kyle commanded.

Rex sat, but he wiggled and barked. Lucky started pulling at his leash and jumping around. He managed to wrap the leash around Drew's legs.

"What's his problem?" Drew asked as he untangled his feet. "He didn't do this yesterday. If Lucky acts like this tomorrow, my parents are not going to be impressed."

"Maybe Rex and Lucky just need a break," Kyle said. "They've been training all week."

Drew frowned. "But Lucky won't get another chance with my parents if he misbehaves tomorrow," he said.

"Think about it. We get weekends off from school, right?" Kyle said. "If Lucky has fun today, maybe he'll be more willing to work tomorrow."

Drew hesitated. Then he unclipped Lucky's leash. "Do you have the ball?" he asked Kyle.

"Yep, right here," Kyle said. He pulled the ball out of his backpack and handed it to Drew. As soon as they saw it, Rex and Lucky started jumping up and down and turning in excited circles.

Drew threw the ball across the park. "Go get it!" he hollered.

Lucky reached the ball before Rex.

"Come, Lucky! Here, boy!" Drew hollered.

Lucky immediately turned and raced back to Drew. Both boys cheered happily as he dropped the ball at Drew's feet. It seemed like the training had paid off.

Kyle didn't know Drew's parents, and he didn't know how Lucky would behave tomorrow. But he knew one thing for sure — Drew and Lucky belonged together. Somehow, they had to show Drew's parents that the dog deserved to stay.

Even if he gets into trouble sometimes, Kyle thought. *Like Rex.*

Decision Day

Kyle and Mia headed over to Drew's house early Saturday morning. Rex trotted along between them.

"Aren't you worried Lucky will act up if Rex is around?" Mia asked.

"Not if I make him sit," Kyle said, grinning. "That's the one thing he does perfectly."

"I hope it's enough," Mia said.

Kyle hoped so, too. Rex's perfect sit-and-stay routine in the clinic waiting room had impressed his mom. Rex was allowed back in the clinic again, but he had to behave.

I just hope Drew's parents are as impressed, Kyle thought.

They pushed open the gate to the backyard. Drew was sitting at the picnic table and looking worried. Nearby, Lucky chased a butterfly around the yard.

"Hey, Drew!" Mia said.

"Hey, guys," Drew replied. "Thanks for coming over."

"Did your parents decide if you can keep Lucky yet?" Kyle asked.

Drew shook his head. "I was waiting for you guys to get here," he said.

"We're here!" Mia exclaimed brightly.

"Then let's get it over with," Drew said. "I'll be right back."

Kyle sat down at the picnic table, and Rex stretched out by his feet. Lucky immediately ran over to greet them. Mia petted Lucky, and he sat beside her.

Drew opened the kitchen door and stuck his head inside. "Mom! Dad!" he called. "Can you come out here for a minute?"

Mr. and Mrs. Martin stepped out onto the patio.

"What's going on?" Drew's dad asked.

"You said Lucky had to start behaving or he'd have to go back to the shelter today," Drew said.

Mr. Martin frowned. He looked confused. "But I —"

Drew kept talking. "Kyle's been helping me train Lucky," he said. "I want to show you what he's learned."

Drew's mom smiled and nudged his dad. "We'd love to see that," she said. "Wouldn't we, honey?"

Drew's dad nodded. "Of course," he said.

Drew's parents both sat down at the picnic table with Kyle and Mia. Drew clipped a leash to Lucky's collar.

"Okay," Drew said. "We're ready."

Kyle took a deep breath and crossed his fingers.

"Please be good," Mia whispered. "Please be good."

Drew started off across the yard. "Heel, Lucky," he said. Lucky hesitated as they walked past Rex, but only for a second.

"Good boy," Drew said when Lucky obeyed. He pulled a treat out of his pocket and fed it to the dog.

Kyle glanced over at Drew's parents. When Drew stopped and Lucky immediately sat down, his mom and dad exchanged a surprised look.

Drew repeated the heel-and-sit exercise two more times. Then he took the leash off and walked back toward the patio. Lucky started to follow, but another butterfly caught his attention. He took off chasing after it.

"Oh, no!" Drew's mom exclaimed as Lucky headed straight for her flower garden. The flowers would be trampled!

Drew's eyes opened wide. "Come! Come, Lucky! Come here, boy!" he shouted.

Lucky stopped and looked back at Drew. He seemed torn between catching the butterfly and listening to his owner.

Drew patted his leg. "Come on, boy!" he called encouragingly.

Kyle and Mia held their breath. They both let out sighs of relief when Lucky ran to Drew.

"Good boy!" Drew said. He knelt down and hugged the dog. Lucky wiggled with happiness and covered him with dog kisses.

"Well!" Drew's dad said, standing up, "that was quite a demonstration."

"I can't believe you taught Lucky so much," his mom added.

Drew grinned. "I had help," he said. "Kyle's a great dog trainer."

"It was mostly Drew," Kyle said. "He worked really hard with Lucky."

"And Lucky is a really smart dog," Mia added.

"How did you teach him to stay out of the trash?" Drew's dad asked.

"I didn't," Drew said. "But I've been taking it out every night so he can't get into it."

Drew's dad looked at Mrs. Martin and laughed. "I thought you were taking the trash out," he said.

"I thought you were!" Mrs. Martin said with a laugh. She looked at Drew. "Did you put my shoes away so Lucky couldn't chew them?"

"Yeah." Drew nodded and sighed. "I have to bribe Lucky with treats, and he doesn't come every time I call. He steals toilet paper rolls and chases butterflies through the garden. He's not perfect, but he's my dog and I want to keep him."

"We don't expect Lucky to be perfect," Drew's mom said. "We just want you to take some responsibility for him."

"I'm sorry, Drew," his dad said, shaking his head. "I was mad when I threatened to take Lucky back to the shelter. I didn't mean it. But I'm so proud of you for working so hard to fix the Lucky problems."

"Then I can keep him?" Drew asked.

"Of course you can," his mom said.

Kyle and Mia stayed to celebrate. The dogs played, and the kids had lemonade and cookies. Mr. Martin wanted to know all about Lucky's training. Drew answered most of his questions.

"Sounds like you're an expert, Drew," his dad said.

"I've been reading a lot," Drew explained with a smile. "It's worth it to get to keep my dog!"

An hour later, Kyle and Mia walked back to the clinic.

"Dr. Blake said Misty is ready to go home," Lillian told them when they walked in. "In fact, I think she can't wait to get out of here. She's in the back room if you want to go see her."

"Great!" Mia said. "I can't wait to have her home."

Kyle and Mia walked to the back room and one of the vet techs set the cat carrier on the table. Misty hissed and spit when she set it down.

"You don't like anyone, do you?" Kyle told the cat with a laugh.

"She likes me," Mia said.

As if to prove her point, the cranky cat purred when Mia scratched her chin through the wire door.

I guess there's a perfect pet for every person, Kyle thought. *They just have to find each other.*

AUTHOR BIO

Diana G. Gallagher lives in Florida with three dogs, eight cats, and a cranky parrot. She has written more than 90 books. When she's not writing, Gallagher likes gardening, garage sales, and spending time with her grandchildren.

ILLUSTRATOR BIO

Adriana Isabel Juárez Puglisi has been a freelance illustrator and writer for more than twenty years and loves telling stories. She currently lives in Granada, Spain, with her husband, son, daughter, two dogs, a little bird, and several fish.

Glossary

agility (uh-JIL-i-tee) — the power of moving quickly and easily

command (kuh-MAND) — to order someone to do something

confident (KON-fuh-duhnt) — having a strong belief in your own abilities

incident (IN-suh-duhnt) — something that happens; an event

irritated (IRH-uh-tay-tid) — upset or annoyed

patient (PAY-shuhnt) — someone who is receiving treatment from a doctor or other health-care provider

resist (ri-ZIST) — to refuse to accept

Discussion Questions

1. What are some other ways Kyle and Mia could have helped Drew with his pet problem? Talk about some different solutions.

2. Do you think Dr. Blake's punishment for Rex was fair? Talk about your opinion.

3. Kyle thinks there is a perfect pet for everyone. Talk about why your pet is perfect for you. If you don't have a pet, talk about what your perfect pet would be.

Writing Prompts

1. Pretend that you're Drew. Write a paragraph to your parents about why you should be able to keep Lucky.

2. Have you ever had to deal with a problem pet? Write a paragraph explaining what the problem was and how you dealt with it.

3. What do you think the best part of having a pet is? What is the hardest part? Write a paragraph about each.

Tips for Training Your Dog

Training your dog is important for many reasons. It's fun to do tricks and show off, but most importantly, it teaches your dog to listen to you. Here are some training tips to get you and your pet started.

- Be consistent — Make sure to use the same words, phrases, and commands every time. Get other family members involved too, so everyone is on the same page. Consistency is the key to success when it comes to training your pet.

- Be firm — Tell your dog what to do in a clear, calm, firm voice so he learns to recognize what you're saying as a command.

- Be affectionate — Make sure to give your dog lots of love when it does something right. You want training to be a fun experience, not a scary one. Being affectionate will make training easier and more fun for you and your pup.

- Be generous — Give your dog lots of treats when it does something right. That way, your dog will know good behavior is rewarded, and it will want to do it again.

- Be patient — Remember that training a dog takes time and work. You can't expect immediate results, so be patient with your dog during the process.

Pet Friends Forever

READ THE WHOLE SERIES

and learn more about
Kyle and Mia's animal adventures!

Find them all at
www.capstonepub.com

Pete&Friends Forever
A No-Sneeze Pet
by Diana G. Gallagher

Pete&Friends Forever
The Great Kitten Challenge
by Diana G. Gallagher

Pete&Friends Forever
Mice Capades
by Diana G. Gallagher

Pete&Friends Forever
The Doggone Dog
by Diana G. Gallagher

Pete&Friends Forever
Problem Pup
by Diana G. Gallagher

Pete&Friends Forever
The Pet Store Pet Show
by Diana G. Gallagher